# Who would steal something on such a snowy day?

"Did you lock the windows last night?" Dr. Prell asked Mrs. Bell.

"I didn't have to. I haven't opened them in weeks," Mrs. Bell said. "It's too cold to open the windows."

Dr. Prell went to the window closest to Eric's, Cam's, and Danny's desks. She pulled at it. The window was locked.

"But look at the footprints," Beth said. "Someone went in and out through there."

"It's locked now," Dr. Prell told Beth. "And if Mrs. Bell says it was locked before, then it was."

Danny pulled at the window. "Hm," he said. "Someone went in and out through the window with the computers. When he was done, he locked the window from the outside and ran off. That's some trick."

"It can't be done," Cam said. "You can't lock the window from the outside."

"And we'll never get those computers back," Danny said. "We'll never solve this mystery."

"Oh, yes we will," Eric said.

# Cam Jansen

## The Snowy Day
## Mystery

**David A. Adler**

Illustrated by Susanna Natti

PUFFIN BOOKS

PUFFIN BOOKS
Published by the Penguin Group
Penguin Young Readers Group,
345 Hudson Street, New York, New York 10014, U.S.A.
Penguin Group (Canada), 90 Eglinton Avenue East, Suite 700, Toronto, Ontario, Canada M4P 2Y3
(a division of Pearson Penguin Canada Inc.)
Penguin Books Ltd, 80 Strand, London WC2R 0RL, England
Penguin Ireland, 25 St Stephen's Green, Dublin 2, Ireland
(a division of Penguin Books Ltd)
Penguin Group (Australia), 250 Camberwell Road, Camberwell, Victoria 3124, Australia
(a division of Pearson Australia Group Pty Ltd)
Penguin Books India Pvt Ltd, 11 Community Centre, Panchsheel Park,
New Delhi - 110 017, India
Penguin Group (NZ), Cnr Airborne and Rosedale Roads, Albany, Auckland 1310, New Zealand
(a division of Pearson New Zealand Ltd)
Penguin Books (South Africa) (Pty) Ltd, 24 Sturdee Avenue, Rosebank,
Johannesburg 2196, South Africa

Registered Offices: Penguin Books Ltd, 80 Strand, London WC2R 0RL, England

First published in the United States of America by Viking,
a division of Penguin Young Readers Group, 2004
Published by Puffin Books, a division of Penguin Young Readers Group, 2005

7  9  10  8  6

Text copyright © David Adler, 2004
Illustrations copyright © Susanna Natti, 2004
All rights reserved

THE LIBRARY OF CONGRESS HAS CATALOGED THE VIKING EDITION AS FOLLOWS:
Adler, David A.
Cam Jansen and the snowy day mystery / David Adler ; illustrated by Susanna Natti.
p.   cm.—(Cam Jansen ; 24)
Summary: Using her photographic memory Cam Jansen joins Eric in solving the
mystery of how some of the school computers were stolen.
ISBN: 0-670-05922-6 (hc)
[ 1. Schools—Fiction.  2. Memory—Fiction.  3. Mystery and detective stories.]
I. Natti, Susanna, ill.  II. Title.
PZ7.A2615Caq1 2004
[Fic]—dc22  2004001643

Puffin Books ISBN 0-14-240417-9

Printed in the United States of America
Set in New Baskerville

For Dad.
Happy ninetieth birthday.
—D.A.

# Chapter One

"It's only snow! It's just tiny flakes!" Mrs. Lane, the school bus driver, shouted. She turned. "Look outside," she told the children on her bus. "It's snowing. So what? I'll tell you so what! Parents drive their children to school when it snows. They block the road, and I can't get this bus close enough to drop you off."

Cam Jansen sat next to the window. She looked out. There was a long line of cars ahead of the bus, and lots of parents were walking with their children to school.

Cam's friend Eric Shelton sat next to her. "We'll be late," Eric said.

"Lots of children will be late," Cam said.

The car just ahead stopped. A man got out. He opened a large umbrella. Then he opened the back door of his car and helped his son out.

Mrs. Lane stuck her head out her window and called to him, "It's only snow! It's just tiny flakes!"

"I'll be right back," the man said.

"No! No!" Mrs. Lane shouted. "Move your car."

The man didn't move his car. He held onto his son's hand and walked with him toward the school.

Mrs. Lane threw up her hands.

"She's upset," Eric whispered.

"She gets upset a lot," Cam said. "But there's a whole line of cars ahead. Umbrella Man couldn't move his car. That's why he got out."

Eric leaned across Cam and looked out

2

the window. "Wow!" he said. "Look at all those cars. We'll be here a while."

*Honk! Honk!*

"Now look!" Mrs. Lane said. "Everyone stopped to let a car come out from the back of the school."

Mrs. Lane turned off the bus engine. She watched as everyone let the car pass. "While we wait," Eric said, "let's have some fun. Let's play a memory game."

Cam looked at the children sitting in the bus. She blinked her eyes and said, *"Click!"* Then she looked outside at all the cars. She blinked her eyes again and said, *"Click!"*

"Close your eyes," Eric said.

Cam closed her eyes.

Eric looked at the girl sitting across the aisle and asked, "What is Patti wearing?"

"A green coat," Cam said with her eyes still closed. "And she has a blue stocking cap and striped mittens on." Cam leaned close to Eric and whispered, "She has the mittens on the wrong hands."

Eric looked at Patti. She did have the mittens on the wrong hands!

"She has a Three Little Pigs lunch box," Cam said. "And the Big Bad Wolf is wearing a blue stocking cap, too, just like Patti."

Cam's friends say she has a mental camera. Adults call it a photographic memory. They mean she remembers just about everything she sees. It's as if she has photographs stored in her head. When Cam wants to remember something, she looks at it, blinks her eyes, and says, *"Click!"* Cam says that's the sound her mental camera makes.

Cam's real name is Jennifer Jansen. When she was a baby, people called her "Red" because she has red hair. But when they found out about her amazing memory, they called her "The Camera." Soon "The Camera" became just "Cam."

Eric asked, "What color car is stopped in front of us?"

"It's yellow, and its license plate is MV613. In front of that is a red car and then a white car, and their license plates are 18CH54 and AI7218. And the car that came from the back of the school is blue, and its license plate is BMY241."

"Wow!" Eric said. "You're amazing."

"Thank you. Thank you," Cam said, and opened her eyes.

Cam looked out the window.

"Hey look," she said. "Umbrella Man is back. The car ahead of his is moving."

The man closed his umbrella.

"Get in," Mrs. Lane called to the man. "Get in your car and move it."

Umbrella Man opened his car door and got in. He turned on the engine and his car moved ahead.

Mrs. Lane drove the bus up to the front of the school. She pushed a button and the bus door opened.

"Good-bye. Good-bye. Have a good day in class," Mrs. Lane said to the children as they got off the bus.

"We're late," Eric told Cam. "Let's hurry."

Eric ran ahead. He slipped on the wet snowy walk. Cam helped him up.

"Let's go," Eric said. "I'm not hurt."

"I'll go," Cam said. "But I'll go slowly."

Cam and Eric walked slowly into school.

# Chapter Two

The front hall of the school was crowded with children and their parents. The principal, Dr. Prell, was there, too.

"Please, be careful," Dr. Prell told people as they walked past her. "The floor is wet. It's slippery."

Cam and Eric passed the office and turned right. They walked past the gym to Room 118. Their teacher, Ms. Benson, stood by the door.

"Good morning, Jennifer. Good morning, Eric," she said as they walked in. A few children were in their seats. Others were still taking off their coats and boots.

Danny took two black checkers from the game corner and a carrot from his lunch bag. He put the checkers over his eyes and scrunched his face to keep them in place. He held the carrot by his nose and called out, "Look at me. I'm a snowman."

"Danny," Ms. Benson said. "Please, get in your seat."

Danny put away his snowman things. "Hey!" he called out as he went to his seat. "This is terrible. There's a radiator here, and I'm melting!"

Danny pretended to be a melting snowman. He wiggled and slowly fell to the floor.

Beth was in her seat right behind Danny's. "You're not funny," she told him. Cam's and Eric's seats were next to each other in the back of the room. Ms. Benson checked who was in class and who was absent.

"Good morning," a voice called out through the speaker on the wall. "This is Dr. Prell. Please listen to the morning announcements."

The children listened. When the announcements were done, Ms. Benson told them, "Get in line, class. We're going to the computer room."

"We have to get in line to get on line," Danny said.

No one laughed.

"Don't you get it?" Danny asked. "You use

a computer to get on line and connect to the Internet."

"We get it," Beth said. "It's just not funny."

"Oh yeah?" Danny said. "Do you know why the cat was thrown out of the computer room? He played with the mouse. And do you know why the hamburger went to the computer store? It went to get chips. Do you get it? Chips! Computer chips, not potato chips."

Beth frowned.

"Do you know why the old man on the mountain stopped to rest on the way to the computer store? He stopped because it was a hard drive. *A hard drive!*"

Danny laughed.

"Don't you get it? He was driving on a mountain road, so it was a hard drive. But there's a hard drive in a computer."

"Stop!" Beth said. "Just stop!"

The children followed Ms. Benson to the computer room.

"Welcome," the computer teacher, Mrs.

Bell, said. "Take your regular seats. Then follow the directions on the board."

Danny pushed to the head of the line. He hurried to his seat by the window. The other children went to their seats.

"Hey," Danny called out. "My computer is missing."

"When will you stop?" Beth asked him. "You're really not funny."

"But it is missing. It really is."

"Mine is gone, too," Eric said.

"So is mine," Cam said.

Mrs. Bell went to Danny's, Eric's, and Cam's desks. Their computers were gone.

"Maybe someone borrowed them," Eric said.

"Maybe they're being fixed," Cam said.

Mrs. Bell shook her head and hurried to the front of the room. She used the room telephone and called the office.

"Let me speak to Dr. Prell."

Mrs. Bell waited. Then she asked, "Did you let someone borrow three of my computers?"

Mrs. Bell listened for a moment and then said, "Well they're gone. Three computers are gone."

"They're stolen," Danny said. "I bet someone stole Mrs. Bell's computers."

# Chapter Three

Mrs. Bell looked by her desk. "Oh, no!" she called out. "The printer is gone, too. It's brand new."

"No, it's not," Beth said. "Someone moved it. It's right here on the floor."

"But why would a thief do that?" Eric asked. "Why would someone steal three computers and leave a brand-new printer?"

Cam looked at the printer. Then she looked at Beth's computer.

"The printer is real big. It's a lot bigger than the computers," Cam said.

Cam looked at the door and then at the windows. "The printer would fit through the doorway, but not through an open window," she said. "So that's what the thief must have done. He took the computers through the window and couldn't get the printer through."

Eric went to the window closest to his desk.

"Look," he said. "Footprints."

Cam went to Eric's window. She looked at the footprints in the snow, blinked her eyes, and said, *"Click!"*

Everyone in Cam's class went to the windows and looked out, including Mrs. Bell.

"Look near all the other windows," Eric said. "None of the others have footprints. This is the only one, and this is where the stolen computers were, so Cam must be right."

Dr. Prell walked into the classroom.

"Over here," Mrs. Bell said. "Three keyboards, towers with CD-ROMs, monitors, and lots of cables were taken."

Danny told Dr. Prell, "The thief came in through the window and he went out with Mrs. Bell's computers."

"I don't think so," Cam said.

"But you just said he did," Danny said.

"Did you lock the windows last night?" Dr. Prell asked Mrs. Bell.

"I didn't have to. I haven't opened them in weeks," Mrs. Bell said. "It's too cold to open the windows."

Dr. Prell went to the window closest to Eric's, Cam's, and Danny's desks. She pulled at it. The window was locked.

"But look at the footprints," Beth said. "Someone went in and out through there."

"It's locked now," Dr. Prell told Beth. "And if Mrs. Bell says it was locked before, then it was."

Danny pulled at the window. "Hm," he said. "Someone went in and out through the window with the computers. When he was done, he locked the window from the outside and ran off. That's some trick."

"It can't be done," Cam said. "You can't lock the window from the outside."

"And we'll never get those computers

back," Danny said. "We'll never solve this mystery."

"Oh, yes we will," Eric said.

Cam looked at the window. She looked at the ceiling, the floor, and the door to Mrs. Bell's room. There were no marks on the ceiling and none of the tiles were missing.

The floor was clean and dry. Everything looked just the way it always did. Beth went to the chalkboard. "We'll make a list of clues," she said. "The first clues are all those footprints by the window."

Beth wrote: *1. Footprints* on the chalkboard.

"Someone should go outside and measure the prints," Eric said, "before they fill up with snow. Then we'll know how big the thief's feet are. That's a clue, too."

"I'll go out," Danny said.

"No, you won't," Dr. Prell told him. "You'll stay right here."

Beth wrote: *2. Locked window* on the board.

"That's a clue, too," she said. "It means

the thief could not have left through the window because he couldn't lock it from the outside."

"Let's check for fingerprints," Eric said. "There must be some on our desks and on the window."

Cam shook her head. "Our hands have been all over our desks. And we all went to the window. Dr. Prell and Danny tried to open it. We'll find lots of fingerprints, our fingerprints," Cam said.

"This is hopeless," Danny said. "I'll never get my computer back."

"Oh, yes, we will," Eric said. "Cam is great at solving mysteries. She once caught someone who stole a bunch of diamonds. She caught people who stole dinosaur bones, gold coins, a Babe Ruth baseball, monkeys, and CDs. She'll catch the computer thief. I'm sure she will."

"Please, come with me," Dr. Prell said to Cam and Eric.

Cam, Eric, and Danny followed Dr. Prell to the door.

"Why are you here?" Dr. Prell asked Danny.

"You said, 'Come with me.'"

"I didn't say that to you," Dr. Prell told Danny. Then she asked, "You didn't do anything wrong, did you?"

"Not this time," Danny said.

"His computer is missing," Mrs. Bell said, "so he can't do his work."

"Okay, Danny, come with me. But please,

don't fool around and don't tell me any of your jokes. I'm not in any mood to laugh about chickens and roads and all that 'knock, knock, who's there?' business. I want to talk about missing computers."

# Chapter Four

"Why did you say I'd find the computers?" Cam asked Eric as they followed Dr. Prell to her office. "I don't know where they are."

"You think she's good at solving mysteries," Danny said to Eric as they followed Dr. Prell to her office. "Well, I have a mystery she can't solve. I bet she can't tell me what I'm thinking right now."

Eric told Danny, "I bet she can."

"Oh, yeah," Danny said. "Go on, Cam. Do that click thing you do and tell me what I'm thinking."

"That's too easy," Cam said. "Right now you think you fooled me."

"Is Cam right?" Eric asked.

Danny nodded.

"And you're thinking of some dumb joke," Eric added. "Right?"

"Yeah," Danny said, "but it's not dumb. It's about an orange that stopped in the middle of the road. Do you know why it stopped? It ran out of juice, that's why."

"I was right," Eric said. "You were thinking of a dumb joke."

Cam, Eric, and Danny followed Dr. Prell

to her office. Mrs. Wayne, the principal's secretary, greeted them. Then she whispered to Danny, "What did you do now?"

"Nothing," Danny said. "I'm here to help Dr. Prell solve a mystery."

"Really! Do you know what he did last year?" Mrs. Wayne asked Cam and Eric. "Last year he walked all over the class bumping into things and shouting 'I can't see! I can't see!' He couldn't see because his eyes were closed."

"That was a good one," Danny said, and smiled.

"Last year," Mrs. Wayne said, "Danny was in this office more than I was."

"Well, I'm not in trouble today," Danny said.

The children went into Dr. Prell's office. They sat on the chairs by her desk and waited while she called the police and reported the crime. Then Dr. Prell said, "The police will be here soon. While we wait, tell me what you know about the missing computers."

"Let me go first," Danny said, "before Cam or Eric reads my mind and tells you everything I'm thinking."

Danny folded his arms. He looked up and said slowly, "I'm thinking the thief has a real strong magnet and used it to lock and unlock the window from the outside. Then, he's real skinny, so he could climb in and out with all those computers. So what we have to do is tell the police to look for a skinny man carrying a large magnet and lots of computers."

"Cam and Eric," Dr. Prell asked, "what do you think happened?"

"It's snowing outside, and the floor of Mrs. Bell's room is dry," Cam said. "That's how I know the thief did not go in and out through the window. There were two thieves, one on the inside who handed the computers out the window to the one on the outside."

"What else do you think?" Dr. Prell asked.

"The computers were stolen just before school. I know that because when we got into the room we could still see footprints in the snow outside the window. It's still snowing, and if the computers were taken in the middle of the night, the footprints would have been completely filled in with snow."

"That's just what I was thinking," Danny said.

"Someone was in the building this morning," Cam said. "He got into Mrs. Bell's room, opened the window, and handed the computers to someone waiting outside."

"Lots of people were here," Dr. Prell said.

"Lots of parents brought their children to school."

*Ring! Ring!*

Dr. Prell picked up her telephone. She listened and then said, "Send them in."

Two police officers walked into the office. One was a tall woman, and one was a not-so-tall man with a short beard.

"I'm Officer Oppen," the not-so-tall officer told Dr. Prell. "Please take us to the scene of the crime."

"There were two thieves," Danny told the police officers as they all walked to Mrs. Bell's room. "They took the computers this morning, just when we were all coming to school."

"Hey," Eric whispered to Cam. "He's taking credit for everything you figured out."

"I don't care," Cam whispered. "I just want Mrs. Bell to get her computers back."

# Chapter Five

"I'm Brenda Davis," the very tall police officer told Mrs. Bell.

"And I'm Gil Oppen," the other officer said. "Where were the computers?"

Mrs. Bell showed the officers Eric's, Cam's, and Danny's desks. The officers looked at the desks, and the children's computers that had not been stolen, the printer, and the windows. Then they looked through the window.

"The footprints lead to the parking lot," Officer Oppen said. "Then they stop."

He opened the window and saw the opening was too small for anyone to climb through.

"How many ways are there out of the building?" Officer Davis asked.

"There's the front door," Dr. Prell said. "There are also doors in the gym and a back door."

Officer Oppen said, "Let's take a look at them."

The two police officers followed Dr. Prell out of the classroom.

Cam, Eric, and Danny sat at their desks.

"Interesting," Danny said, "very interesting." He pretended to be working on his missing computer.

"Stop it," Beth told him. "Look at Mrs. Bell. She doesn't think any of this is funny."

Mrs. Bell stood by the door. Her arms were folded. Her head was down. Many of the children in the class were talking, but Mrs. Bell seemed too upset to notice.

"Hello! Hello!" Ms. Benson called from the door.

Mrs. Bell looked up.

"It's time for my children to come back to class," Ms. Benson said.

"Not yet," Mrs. Bell said. "I have to tell you what happened." She told Ms. Benson about the stolen computers.

Ms. Benson said, "You should check if anything else was taken."

"I have a good pen in my desk and coins for the coffee machine," Mrs. Bell said. She hurried to her desk and opened the top drawer. "It's all here, the pen and the coins."

The children followed Ms. Benson to Room 118. They all sat in their seats.

"I tried to help solve the crime," Danny told Ms. Benson, "but the thief is smart. Somehow, without anyone seeing him, he got the computers out of the building."

"He's wrong," Cam whispered to Eric. "Someone must have seen him. If he came in the front door, Dr. Prell saw him, but she probably thought he was a parent who brought his child to school."

"What if he came in through the gym or the back door?"

"Let's go find out," Cam said.

Cam and Eric went to Ms. Benson.

"May we leave the room for a few minutes?" Cam asked.

"It's about the stolen computers," Eric told her.

"Go ahead," Ms. Benson said.

Cam and Eric went to the gym first. Mr. Day, the gym teacher, was there setting up the volleyball net.

Cam pointed to the two large doors on the other side of the gym and asked, "Did anyone come in or leave through there this morning?"

Mr. Day said, "Dr. Prell and the police were

just here. They were the only ones who opened those doors today."

Cam and Eric walked to the other side of the gym. Cam opened the doors and looked outside.

"Look at the snow," Cam whispered. "Mr. Day is right."

The field behind the gym was covered with a smooth blanket of snow.

"There are no footprints," Cam told Eric. "No one has been back here this morning."

"It's cold," Mr. Day shouted. "Please, close the door!"

Cam closed it. "Now, let's check the back door," she said.

Cam and Eric walked through the lunchroom and kitchen and into the custodian's office. Mrs. Adams, the custodian, was sitting at her desk. Just beyond her desk was a large door.

"Hi, Cam. Hi, Eric," Mrs. Adams said.

Cam asked her, "Did anyone come in through here before school started?"

"Two police officers just asked me the same question," Mrs. Adams said. "I'll tell you what I told them. Lots of teachers park their cars and come in through here every morning. They come in early, before the children."

"Just teachers?" Cam asked.

"Yes. Just teachers. I sit here to be sure no one else comes in."

Cam opened the door.

"Look at all those footprints," Eric said.

"I'm not looking for footprints," Cam said. "I'm looking for something else."

Cam looked across the parking lot.

"We have to go outside for a minute," Cam said to Mrs. Adams. "Will you let us back in?"

"Of course I will, but hurry."

Cam and Eric stepped outside. The door closed behind them.

# Chapter Six

Cam walked quickly into the parking lot. Eric followed her.

"What are we looking for?" Eric asked.

Cam said, "I need to know how the thieves got away with three computers. I know one thief passed them through the window. But the thief outside couldn't just walk away carrying three computers."

"Maybe he took them to his car," Eric said, "and then drove away with them."

Cam and Eric walked through the parking lot. It was on the side of the building. Then Cam stopped.

"There's Mrs. Bell's room," Cam said.

"Look at all the cars here," Eric said. "Maybe the computers are still here, in one of the cars."

Cam turned and looked at the many cars parked in the teachers' lot.

"Maybe they're hidden in someone's trunk," Eric said.

Cam thought for a moment. Then she pointed to the left and said, "That's the way out of the lot." Then she pointed to the right and asked, "What's that way?"

Cam walked to the right.

"Mrs. Adams can tell us that," Eric said. "Let's go inside. I'm cold."

Cam kept walking.

"I'm really cold," Eric said. "Look! I can see my breath."

Eric exhaled, and a small foggy cloud appeared.

"You can go in," Cam told him.

Cam continued to walk to the right, and Eric followed her.

The lot led to the back of the building.

"It ends right here," Cam said. "If the thieves put the computers in their car, they would have to go out the other way, past the front of the building. Someone must have seen them drive by."

"Lots of people saw them," Eric said. "Don't you remember? There were lots of cars here this morning and lots of parents who came with their children. They must have all seen the thieves."

"Yes," Cam said as she and Eric walked

to the back door. "The thieves got lost in the crowd."

Cam knocked on the back door.

"Maybe the thieves are still here," Eric said.

Mrs. Adams opened the door. She felt Cam's hands.

"Oh, my," she said. "You must be freezing. Sit here for a minute and warm up."

Mrs. Adams had a small electric heater set on the floor by her desk. Cam and Eric sat next to it.

"You're trying to find the missing computers, aren't you?" Mrs. Adams asked.

"Yes," Cam said.

Eric rubbed his hands near the heater. He took off his shoes and put his feet near the heater, too.

"This feels good," Eric said.

"Would you like some pretzels?" Mrs. Adams asked.

"Thank you," Eric said, and took a few pretzels. He stretched out.

Cam took a pretzel, too. When she was

done eating it she told Eric, "Put on your shoes. We have to get back to class."

Eric put on his shoes. He and Cam thanked Mrs. Adams. Then they walked back to class.

"I still think the computers might be in one of the cars," Eric said while they were walking in the hall. "Maybe a teacher stole them and hid them in his trunk. When school is over, he'll take them home."

Cam shook her head and said, "I don't think one of the teachers would steal from the school. Anyway, it would take two teachers to steal the computers, one in Mrs. Bell's class and one outside. I really don't think *two* teachers would steal from the school."

Cam opened the door to Room 118. The children were all seated quietly. They were writing in their journals.

Cam and Eric sat in their seats. Cam opened her journal. She wrote in it all about Mrs. Bell's computers. Then she stopped writing.

"Oh, my," she said.

Cam closed her eyes and said, *"Click!"* She said, *"Click!"* again.

"Oh, my," she said again and opened her eyes. "That's it!"

# Chapter Seven

"What's it?" Eric whispered.

"I know how to catch the computer thieves," Cam answered. "I'm sure I do."

Eric said, "You have to tell Mrs. Bell and Dr. Prell. You have to tell Officer Oppen and Officer Davis."

Cam closed her eyes and said, *"Click!"*

"Why are you clicking?" Eric asked. "I thought you already solved the mystery."

Cam didn't answer. Instead, she said, *"Click!"* again. With her eyes closed, she wrote in her journal. Then she opened her eyes, looked at what she had written, and told Eric, "Let's go."

Cam took her journal. Then she and Eric went to Ms. Benson. Cam told her, "We need to leave the room. We need to speak to Dr. Prell."

"But you just came back."

"This is important," Eric said. "Cam knows how to find Mrs. Bell's computers."

"Promise me," Ms. Benson said, "that you'll spend some time in class today."

"We promise," Eric said.

Cam and Eric left the room.

"Wait! Wait!" Danny called to them. "I'm going, too."

Danny was at the door. Ms. Benson was right behind him.

"And just where are you going?" Ms. Benson asked.

"It was my computer that was stolen. We're all going to help catch the thieves." Danny smiled. He pointed to his head and said, "You know, I have some good ideas in here, some real good ideas."

"Don't fool around," Ms. Benson told Danny. Then she let him go, too.

In the hall Eric pointed to Danny's head and said, "I think all you have in there are bad jokes."

"That's not true. I have good jokes in here. Lots of them."

Cam, Eric, and Danny hurried to the office. "We need to see Dr. Prell," Eric told Mrs. Wayne, the principal's secretary.

Mrs. Wayne asked, "What did Danny do?"

"Nothing," Danny said.

"Was there a fight? Is someone hurt? Is someone sick?" Mrs. Wayne asked.

"No," Danny said. "It's about the computers."

"Oh," Mrs. Wayne said. She looked to be sure no one else was listening. Then she leaned forward and whispered, "Did you know some computers were stolen?"

"Yes," Eric said, "and Cam knows how to catch the people who took them."

"Oh," Mrs. Wayne said. "You should tell that to Dr. Prell."

Mrs. Wayne picked up the handset to her telephone. She pushed a button and told Dr. Prell that Cam, Eric, and Danny wanted to see her. She listened for a moment and then said, "You may go right in."

Dr. Prell was sitting by her desk.

Cam told her, "The thieves drove off with the computers in the trunk of their blue car."

"How do you know that?" Dr. Prell asked.

"This morning—" Cam began.

"Oh, it doesn't matter how you know," Dr. Prell said, "and it doesn't help. There must be hundreds, maybe thousands of blue cars in this town."

Cam opened her journal. "But only one," Cam said, "with the license plate BMY241."

Dr. Prell picked up the handset to her telephone. "I'm calling the police," she said. She started to dial the telephone. Then she stopped. "No," she said. "First tell me how you know who took the computers."

"Yes," Danny said. "How do you know?"

"When all those parents came in with their children this morning, a thief came in, too. He went to Mrs. Bell's room, opened the window, and passed three computers to someone waiting outside."

"Yeah," Danny said. "And one of those computers was mine."

"The thieves didn't carry those computers away," Cam said. "They couldn't. Someone would have seen them."

"And they're heavy," Eric said. "So the

thief outside carried them to their car. It was in the parking lot. The parking lot is on the side of the building, so no one saw them."

"What about the teachers?" Danny asked.

"They came to school earlier," Cam said.

"But how do you know it's a blue car?" Dr. Prell asked, "and how do you know the license plate number?"

"I can tell you that," Eric said. "There were lots of cars here this morning. Lots of parents drove their children to school."

"Mine didn't," Danny said. "I came by bus."

"Parents drove to the front of the school," Eric said. "That's where they stopped their cars."

"That's right," Dr. Prell said. "The only people who go in through the back door are teachers."

"But we saw a blue car leave from the back of the school with BMY241 on its license plate. Now, who would leave from the back?" Cam asked.

"The thieves," Danny said. "The thieves!"

Dr. Prell picked up the handset to her telephone again. She called the police. She told Officer Davis about the blue car. Dr. Prell looked at Cam's journal. Then she told Officer Davis to look for a car with the license plate BMY241.

# Chapter Eight

"I wish I had a *Click! Click!* memory," Danny said. "Then I wouldn't forget so many jokes."

"You remember enough," Dr. Prell said.

"Here's one I didn't forget," Danny said. "What goes 'Ha, ha, thud'?"

Dr. Prell, Cam, and Eric didn't answer. Instead Dr. Prell asked Cam, "I'm sure you don't know every car's license plate. How did you remember the one on the blue car?"

"While we were on the bus," Eric said, "we played a memory game. We do that a lot. Cam looks around and *clicks*. She closes her eyes and I quiz her. I ask tough questions, so

Cam tries to remember everything."

"Really," Danny said again. "This is a good one. What goes 'Ha, ha, thud'?"

"Memory games are fun," Dr. Prell said. Then she looked at her watch. "Oh, my. It's almost time for lunch. You should go back to class. I'll let you know if I hear from the police."

"Someone who's laughing his head off," Danny said. "That's what goes 'Ha, ha, thud.'"

"That's very nice," Dr. Prell told Danny. "Now please, go back to class."

Cam, Eric, and Danny left Dr. Prell's office.

"Good-bye," Mrs. Wayne said as they walked through the outer office.

"We did it," Danny whispered to Mrs. Wayne. "Right about now the police are arresting those computer thieves."

"Oh, my," Mrs. Wayne said. "That's wonderful."

When they were in the hall, Danny said, "Here's another good one. How do you send a wig?"

"Do you think the police will catch the thieves?" Eric asked.

"Every car is registered," Cam said. "They just have to check who owns the car with the BMY241 license plate. If it's the thieves' car, if it isn't stolen, they'll catch them."

"You send a wig hair mail. Do you get it?" Danny asked. "It's hair, so you send it hair mail instead of air mail. Here's another one. Do you know why a hummingbird hums? It knows the tune but it doesn't know the words. That's why."

When they came to class, Ms. Benson was teaching a math lesson. Cam, Eric, and Danny sat in their seats and opened their notebooks.

"Copy the homework problems," Ms. Benson said when the lesson was done.

*Rrrr! Rrrr!*

It was time for lunch.

Cam, Eric, and the other children in the class took their lunch bags and boxes from the closet. Then they went to the lunchroom.

Eric unwrapped his sandwich. "Jelly on toast," he told Cam.

"I have American cheese on pumpernickel," Cam said.

"Hey," Danny said, and pointed. "Look! It's Dr. Prell and the police."

Dr. Prell and Officer Oppen and Officer Davis were at the lunchroom door.

"They're looking for someone," Danny said.

Dr. Prell smiled. She spoke to the two police officers. Then they walked toward Cam and Eric's table.

Danny fell to the floor. He got on his knees, held his hands together, and called out, "Please, don't arrest me. I'm innocent, I tell you! I'm innocent!"

"No you're not," Beth said. "You're guilty of telling bad jokes, really bad jokes."

"Officer Oppen has some good news," Dr. Prell said.

"We found the car," Officer Oppen told Cam and Eric. "The computers were still in the trunk."

"We also arrested the thieves," Officer Davis added.

"You deserve a reward," Dr. Prell told Cam and Eric.

"Hey, what about me?" Danny asked. "I helped."

"Get off the floor," Dr. Prell told Danny.

Then she smiled and said to Cam's entire class, "You'll all get rewards."

Dr. Prell went into the kitchen and came out with a large box of ice-cream cups and wooden spoons, enough for everyone.

"Let's celebrate," Dr. Prell said.

Dr. Prell sat at the table with Cam and her friends. She took the lid off a cup of vanilla ice cream and started to eat. Officer Oppen and Officer Davis sat, too, one on each side of Danny, and ate ice cream.

Danny looked to his right at Officer Oppen. He looked to his left at Officer Davis.

Danny pretended to be afraid.

"I'll be good," Danny said. "I promise I'll be good."

"That means no more jokes in class," Beth said.

Danny agreed. "No more jokes."

"Wow!" Beth said, and laughed. "No more of Danny's jokes. That's a real reason to celebrate."

Dr. Prell laughed.

"I want to remember this day, the day Danny stopped telling jokes in class," Cam said.

Cam got up. She took a few steps back. She looked at Dr. Prell, Eric, Danny, the two police officers, Beth, and the others in her class, blinked her eyes again, and said, *"Click!"*

# A Cam Jansen Memory Game

Take another look at the picture opposite page 1. Study it. Blink your eyes and say, *"Click!"* Then turn back to this page and answer these questions. Please, first study the picture, *then* look at the questions.

1. How many buses in the picture?
2. How many cars?
3. How many cars are in front of the bus?
4. How many are behind?
5. Are all the children outside the bus wearing hats?
6. Is it still snowing?
7. Does Mrs. Lane look happy?